A Story of Determination, Resilience, and the Celebration of the Human Spirit!

DEDICATION

To Ken…you put such heart and passion into everything you do.
What Luck to have you for a son! A.M.M.
What Luck to have you for a brother. D.S.M.

To My Bright & Beautiful Grandchildren
Aero & Valentina Kasabach, and Sparrow & Hazel Lecours, who continue to inspire me every day. N.S.

ACKNOWLEDGEMENTS

A special shout-out – to my wonderful husband Jay, my amazing daughters-in-law Caryn and Angeline, and my grandchildren Jaden, Gabrielle, Jenna and Lucas who always make me smile--thank you for listening as we shared our story and for being our biggest fans. To my friends Carole Bernstein, Ellen Brazer, Alexandra Flinn, Tony Fredericks, Chris and Nancy Jennison, Susan Massey and Jennifer Resnick --thank you for sharing perspectives, ideas, and suggestions.
Your creativity and eye for detail are reflected throughout the story. A.M.M.

To my family – my daughters Amanda, Victoria and Vanessa, my sisters Dale Schemer and Cindy Simons Bennett, my parents Irv & Lila Simons (author of *I'm So Magic*) – thank you for the many years of your artistic encouragement. To my supportive and talented husband, Aurelio – you are the wind beneath my wings. N.S.

WhatLuckBooks.com
ISBN: 978-0-578-46259-2
© 2020 What Luck! LLC

ISBN 978-0-578-46259-2
51595
9 780578 462592

What Luck!

By Anita Meyer Meinbach & David Meinbach
Illustrated by Nancy Simons Sica

*"Success is no accident. It is hard work,
perseverance, learning, studying, sacrifice and most of all,
love of what you're doing, or learning to do."*
– Pelé

Kenny jumped out of bed and straightened the blue and white crumpled baseball shirt he always slept in for good luck. **"Today's the day!"** he shouted. Kenny Miller loved baseball. He loved it more than anything, more than his insect collection, or his goldfish Louise, or even his two brown hamsters, Jellybean and Gumdrop.

He picked up his leather baseball glove, brought it to his nose, and inhaled deeply. He LOVED the way it smelled.

He LOVED THE THRILL of rounding the bases and crossing home plate.

Most of all, he LOVED THE SOUND
when the bat and the ball connected with a loud **"CRACK!"**

3

But loving baseball wasn't enough. He dreamed of being a Wildcat and playing for his neighborhood team. First, they said he wasn't old enough, and then they told him he wasn't good enough.

This year would be different.

Kenny spent hours pitching to the bright red bull's-eye painted on the garage door. He spent days throwing balls at an old garbage pail in his backyard, and for months, Kenny practiced catching and hitting. Now, he was ready. **"This year I'll make the team,"** he repeated to himself as he headed to school. **"I just have to!"**

On Monday, all Kenny could think about in class was baseball. Tryouts started right after school. He imagined himself at the plate, wearing the team jersey. He heard the crowd yell his name as he hit the ball out of the park! He was the Jackie Robinson of the Wildcats and the crowd was cheering,

"KENNY!"
"KENNY!"
"KENNY!"

Just then, the crowd's roar faded into the voice of Randy Morgan. "Hey, Shorty, trying out for the team again?" Randy asked. "You'll never make it!"

"I'll show him!" Kenny thought, as he ran home from school to change clothes.

"All I need is a little luck!"

Kenny grabbed his favorite baseball cap and attached the rabbit's foot he had won at the fair. Now Kenny knew he would play well. After all, he had what no one else had - **a lucky rabbit's foot!**

At practice, Kenny stood at the pitcher's mound. His hands were sweaty and his heart pounded. He kicked the dirt, adjusted his cap, and threw the ball.

The batter swung, hitting a grounder right to Kenny. Kenny bent to scoop up the ball. At that instant, the rabbit's foot flopped over his eyes and the ball rolled away.

Coach groaned.

Randy laughed.

"Tomorrow, I'll have to do better, I just need more luck!"

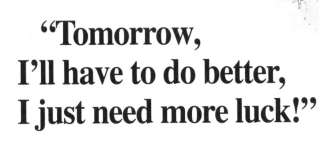

7

On Tuesday, Kenny searched through his coin collection until he found his favorite coin, a bright copper penny his grandfather had given him. He placed the penny in his sneaker and put on his baseball cap with the lucky rabbit's foot attached - pinned to the side.

Now, Kenny was sure that he would play well!

At practice, it was Kenny's turn at bat.
He took a practice swing.
He imagined hitting the ball – a home run!

He stepped up to the plate. The pitcher threw the ball.
Kenny followed its path and swung hard. A loud "crack"
shattered the air!

Moving at lightning speed, he heard Coach shout,

"Run, Miller, Run!"

The shortstop grabbed the ball and threw it
to first, but it sailed over the first baseman's head.

"Run to Second, Miller."
Coach shouted.

Kenny was rounding first when
the penny got caught between his toes.
"Ouch," he cried, limping as fast as he could.
Before he could reach base, Kenny was tagged
out. Coach rolled his eyes.
"Slow-poke," yelled Randy.

**"Tomorrow,
I just need more luck!"**

On Wednesday, Kenny pulled out an old shoe box from under his bed where he hid his most treasured possession - a baseball card of his hero, Jackie Robinson.

He put the card into the sleeve of his shirt, placed the penny in his sneaker –near the heel – and put on his baseball cap with the lucky rabbit's foot attached.

Now, Kenny was confident he would do well!

Today at practice, Kenny was in right field and he wasn't happy. "No ball ever makes it this far," Kenny thought, and reached under his sleeve for his baseball card. **It was gone!**

He searched the ground around him. **It wasn't there!**

"I've lost it," Kenny thought, panic gripping him, **"I've lost it!"**

Finally, out of the corner of his eye, Kenny spotted the card. With a sigh of relief, he bent down to grab it, and missed the fly ball that landed behind him.

"Hey, Shorty," Randy Morgan taunted, "you've got to jump for those!"

Coach frowned and shook his head.

"**Tomorrow**," Kenny sighed.

"I just need more luck!"

On Thursday, Kenny rummaged through his bedroom closet until he found what he was looking for - a crystal on a black cord. He discovered it one day on the way to school. He probably wouldn't have noticed it, but at that second, the light from the sun hit the crystal and created a rainbow of colors. Kenny couldn't stop staring.

It was Magical!

Kenny tied the crystal around his neck, slipped the baseball card into his back pocket, placed the penny in his sneaker, and put on his cap with the lucky rabbit's foot attached. Now Kenny was positive he would play well.

Today he was the catcher!

Kenny put on the catcher's mask, the vest and waddled to home plate.

He put on the catcher's mitt and pounded it with his fist.

He crouched down behind home plate, eyes on the pitcher as he threw a few warm-ups.

The batter walked up to the plate.

The pitch was thrown and the batter swung!

Kenny leaped up and watched the ball as it soared – a high fly ball. As he held out his mitt, ready to catch the ball, the crystal caught the sun's light. The ball disappeared in a swirl of brilliant colors and landed on the ground with a loud thud.

"**Hey, Miller, always keep an eye on the ball!**" Coach yelled.

"**Get some glasses!**" Randy yelled.

"**Next time,**" Kenny sighed,

"I just need more luck."

But Kenny knew time was running out.

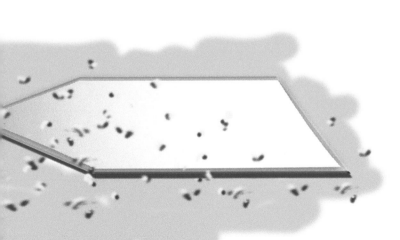

Tomorrow was the last day of tryouts. "I just have to make the team," he thought for the hundredth time. To make matters worse, he knew he couldn't take any more of Randy Morgan's teasing.

"When will you give up?"

Randy demanded each day.

The other kids laughed when Randy told them what happened to Kenny during tryouts.

There was no school on
Friday and Kenny overslept.
He jumped out of bed, dressed,
and rushed out of the house.
Just as the door banged shut, he realized
he had forgotten his lucky charms.
If he went back for them, he would be late
for tryouts and never make the team.
"What luck!" he thought sadly,
and ran to the field, leaving
everything behind.

That morning Kenny fielded without a single error and batted without a single out.

He caught a fly ball – no rabbit's foot to blind him.

He hit a single and stole second base - no penny to pinch his toes.

He tagged out a runner - no crystal to distract him.

For the first time, Coach was smiling and Randy Morgan didn't have a thing to say! Kenny was feeling quite lucky.

At the end of tryouts, Coach announced that on Monday he'd post the names of the new additions to the Wildcat team.

"How can I wait the whole weekend?" Kenny wondered.

"Monday is years away!"

All weekend he thought about how he'd played during tryouts. He knew he had messed up. But Friday was different- Friday he played great! And he did it without the magic of his lucky charms.

He gathered them and examined each one carefully - slowly turning one and then another, over and over, searching for the luck each promised.

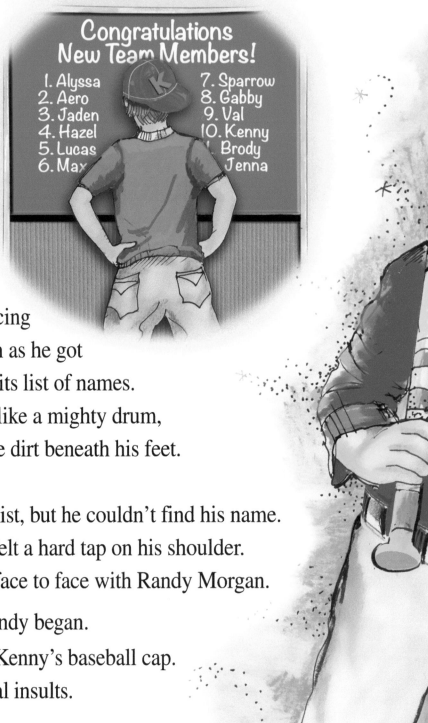

Congratulations
New Team Members!

1. Alyssa
2. Aero
3. Jaden
4. Hazel
5. Lucas
6. Max

7. Sparrow
8. Gabby
9. Val
10. Kenny
    Brody
    Jenna

Monday afternoon, right after school, Kenny ran to the Wildcat's field. His stomach was in knots. A hundred fly balls were bouncing around inside. He slowed down as he got closer to the notice board with its list of names. He could hear his heart pound like a mighty drum, and his mouth was as dry as the dirt beneath his feet. Would his name be there?

Kenny's eyes scanned the list, but he couldn't find his name. He looked again. Just then he felt a hard tap on his shoulder. Kenny spun around and came face to face with Randy Morgan.

"Hey Shorty!" Randy began. He reached out and pulled off Kenny's baseball cap. Kenny waited for Randy's usual insults.

24

"**Here,**" Randy said with a smile, and handed Kenny a brand new Wildcat baseball cap. "You'll need this for practice next week."

Kenny stared in disbelief. "Why is Randy being so nice? What just happened?" He looked down at the cap tightly clasped in his hands. Finally, he found his voice, "**I did it?**" he whispered. "**You did it!**" Randy said, and gave him a high-five. "**Good job, Kenny!**"

25

Kenny raced home, his Wildcat cap sitting proudly on his head, his feet barely touching the ground. His mind was racing too as he thought about the hours, days, and months he had practiced with the red bull's-eye and the old garbage can.

He thought about how he played at tryouts, and he thought about his lucky charms.

"The magic

Slowly, a curious smile crossed his face as a new thought hit him. "I tried to bring myself luck, but the magic is not in the crystal. The magic is not in my Jackie Robinson baseball card, or in my bright copper penny, or even in my lucky rabbit's foot."

At that moment, Kenny knew where the magic really was, where it had always been.

is in me!"

Fun Facts:

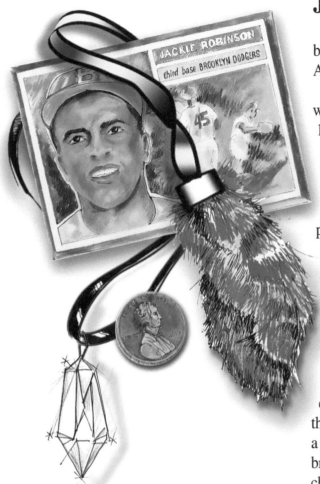

Jackie Robinson (1919-1972)

Jackie Robinson's courage and talent helped him break through the "color barrier" to become the first African American player in the Major Leagues.

He signed with the Brooklyn Dodgers in 1945, won the 'National League Rookie of the Year' Award in 1947 and the "Most Valuable Player" trophy in 1949.

In 1955 he helped the Brooklyn Dodgers win their first World Series Championship.

Jackie Robinson's name is legendary. He believed that with hard work and perseverance, anything is possible. Jackie Robinson's life has inspired generations and generations to fight for what is right and to believe that they can be the change they wish to see.

Good Luck Charms

Good luck charms are those that are believed to bring good luck. While many have been associated with ancient ceremony and culture, good luck charms can be anything that has special significance to the wearer: a found treasure, a reminder of a special place or time, or something that brings a feeling of happiness. Some popular good luck charms include: a four-leaf clover, horseshoe, coin, or a rabbit's foot.

About the Rabbit's Foot: No rabbit was hurt. Just like Kenny in this story, most people who carry a rabbit's foot buy those that are 100% synthetic - made from plastic.

Meet The Authors & Illustrator

Anita Meyer Meinbach, Ed.D

As a parent, classroom teacher, and Associate Professor at the University of Miami's School of Education and Human Development, Anita long recognized the power of children's literature to inspire and transform lives. The author of over a dozen books for educators to help them bring the magic and joy of children's literature into the classroom, she was honored as Miami-Dade Teacher of the Year, 2003, and selected to be on one of *U.S.A. Today's* "All Teacher Team." Anita and her husband Jay live in South Florida.

David Steven Meinbach, MD

A graduate of Northwestern University and the University of Miami School of Medicine, David is a urologist and partner in University Urology in Delray Beach, Florida. David grew up loving books. Together, with his wife Angeline, they have instilled this same love and enthusiasm in their children, Gabrielle and Lucas. The idea for **What Luck!** was an outgrowth of a conversation David and his mom had when reminiscing about the days he spent as a young boy waiting in the outfield for a ball to come his way!

Nancy Simons Sica, Bachelor of Design

A graduate of the University of Florida with a Degree in Advertising & Design. Nancy is an Award-Winning Art Director, Designer and Children's Book Illustrator at Miami's Aurelio & Friends Advertising. She is Executive Vice-President and Business Partner with her husband, Aurelio. They are very proud of their three accomplished daughters...Vanessa, an Industrial Designer, Amanda, a Graphic Designer and Victoria, a Corporate Attorney, as well as grandparents of... *TWO* sets of adorable *TWIN*S –Aero & Valentina, Hazel & Sparrow!

CPSIA information can be obtained
at www.ICGtesting.com
Printed in the USA
BVHW021146100120
569193BV00011B/44/P